This Book belongs to

_____

For my sons Arya and Aayush and my beautiful wife Sujata.

Pronunciation & Culture Guide
Pratham(Pra-TUM) means "First" in Hindi.
Bandhu(Ban-DOO) means "Your friend" in Hindi.
Puri Bhaji(poo-ree paw-ji) is a favorite Indian "comfort food" made of deep fried rounds of flour served with spiced potatoes. Make it at home—recipe in back!.
Holi (pronounced "Holy") is a spring festival of color observed in India. People celebrate with music, games, food, and by throwing colored water or powder at each other.

A Note from the Author

We hope you enjoy "Use Your Words" and we would
love to hear your feedback.
Please post your reviews online.

THANK YOU!

Engage with us on Social Media
Facebook.com/KommuruBooks
www.KommuruBooks.com

ISBN-13: 978-1-946312-01-3

Ramesh and Suresh were two brothers. They both got good grades in school and could speak English, Hindi, and French.

Even though they spoke three languages, they thought it was more fun to speak gibberish.

It was the night before the Holi Festival of Colors.

The brothers came home after playing all day with friends.

"It's time for dinner," Mom said.

Ramesh answered, "Iggy biggy boo."

"What is this gibberish?" asked Mom.

This time Suresh answered, "Biggy boo iggy!"

"Nonsense! Is this what you learn in school?" she asked. "Sit down and eat. It's your favorite, Puri Bhaji."

As they ate, Mom asked, "Ramesh, do you like your food?"

Ramesh giggled and said, "Iggy biggy boo."

A little let down, Mom turned to Suresh and asked, "This is your favorite food, isn't it?"

Suresh smiled and said, "Biggy boo iggy!"

Now Mom was mad. She said,
  "That's it! No games, no music, and you are both
  grounded. Both of you upstairs and in bed right now!"

The brothers walked sadly to their room. But the moment they closed the door, they started bouncing on the bed.

They bounced so hard they broke the bed! The bed started sinking down, but they didn't touch the floor!

The floor opened up, swallowing Ramesh and Suresh in. They screamed at the top of their lungs,

"AAAAHHHHHH!"

They tried to hold on to something, but they kept sliding down a long tunnel.

"AAAAHHHHHH!"

Finally, they landed at the bottom of the tunnel with a THUD.

The brothers got up and looked at the strange, new place.

They held each other's hands and walked around but couldn't find anyone.

After walking for a while, they found themselves back where they started.

Just then, they heard a sound. They turned and saw a funny looking creature looking at them.

"AAAAHHHHHH!"
they screamed.

"AAAAHHHHHH!"
the creature screamed back.

Realizing the creature was also scared of them, the boys stopped screaming.

Ramesh bravely asked, "Who are you?"

The creature replied, "Badabeesh."

Suresh said, "I don't think it speaks English."

He asked in Hindi, "Aap koun hai?"

The creature replied again, "Badabeesh."

"Let's try French," said Ramesh. "Qui etes vous?"

The creature replied yet again, "Badabeesh."

Ramesh looked at Suresh. "The only thing it says is 'badabeesh'!" he laughed.

Suddenly, another creature ran up to them.

It yelled, "Badabeesh, badabeesh, badabeesh!"

Then it bent over and held both of its noses.

They all giggled, and Ramesh said, "I think he's trying to say something."

The creature pointed behind him and yelled again, "Badabeesh, badabeesh, badabeesh!"

Suresh giggled, "I think there is a play area back there and he wants to play."

"Nah, I think he is saying there is a pony ride back there," laughed Ramesh.

As they laughed, two more creatures ran up and threw a bucket of colored water at them.

The gush soaked everyone in water.

"Oh, they're playing Tron games, and he was trying to warn his us!" laughed Ramesh.

The two creatures ran to another bucket and started
pulling it back and forth.

"Badabeesh!" the first one yelled.

"Badabeesh!" the second yelled back.

Then the first creature punched the second one on the nose!

The second creature punched him back. Then punches were flying right and left.

"Oh, no! They're fighting over the water!" Suresh said.

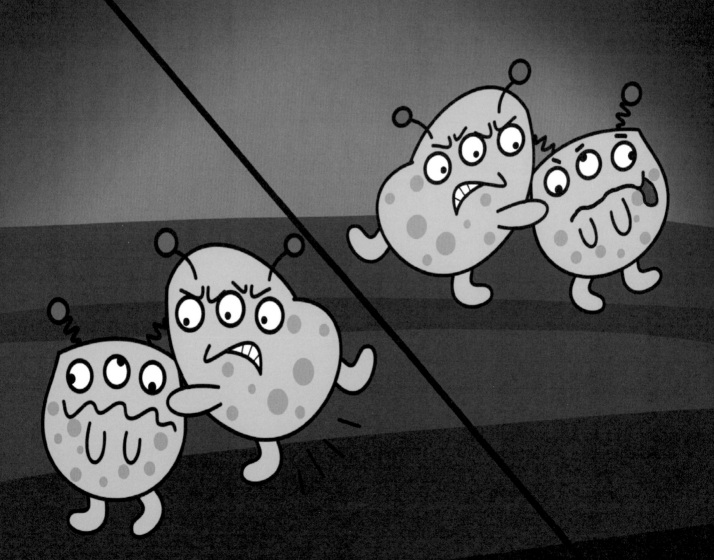

Ramesh ran over and stopped the fight. He filled two water pistols from the bucket and gave one to each creature.

They smiled and said, "Badabeesh! Badabeesh!"

Suresh bust up with laughter. "It's simple if they just talked to each other! But all these guys say is 'Badabeesh'!"

Ramesh and Suresh marched ahead hoping to find someone who could speak English, Hindi, or French.

They walked for a long time into what seemed like the middle of the night. Finally, they saw a stage set with all sorts of drums.

"It looks like the stage is set for Holi songs and celebrations," said Suresh.

A creature stood on the stage with a microphone.

"He must be a rock star!" said Ramesh.

Ramesh and Suresh were tired of hearing gibberish. They were ready for some rock and roll! They ran to the stage and joined everyone sitting in a circle.

The rock star closed his eyes and brought the microphone to his mouth.

Then he opened his eyes and screamed at the top of his lungs,

"BADABEESH, BADABEESH, BADABEESH!"

Ramesh couldn't take it anymore. He stood up and screamed, "STOP! What are you guys doing!?

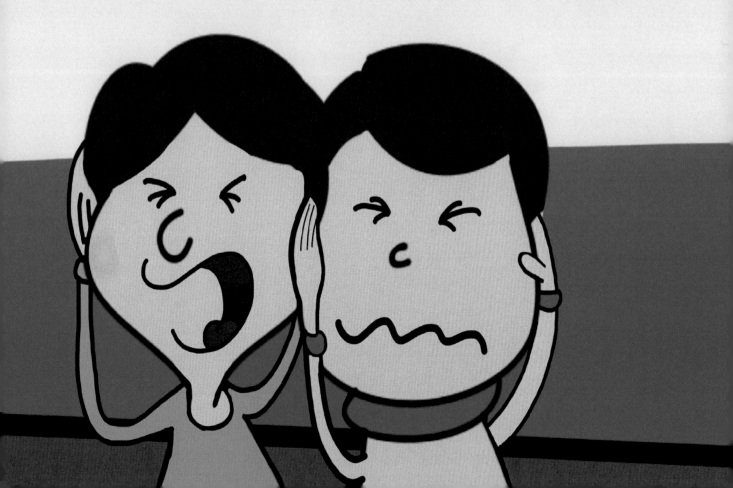

All you do is speak gibberish with your 'badabeesh, badabeesh, badabeesh'! USE YOUR WORDS!"

He looked around, but everyone looked confused. Disappointed, Ramesh put his head down.

Suresh stood up and said, "It's OK. We'll teach you words."

Ramesh started with basics like "hello" and "goodbye."

Suresh taught them manners like "please" and "thank you."

The creatures learned very quickly.

Then Ramesh said, "I am Ramesh. Who are you?"

A creature came forward and said, "I'm the first one you met. You can call me Pratham."

Another came forward and said, "I'm his friend. You can call me Bandhu."

Ramesh asked, "Where are we?"

Pratham replied, "Are you guys lost?"

"Yes," Ramesh said, "And we're missing our friends, school, and …"

"… and Mama and Papa," Suresh added.

Pratham smiled big and said, "Don't worry! I can send you back!"

The brothers jumped up excitedly. "Really?" they asked.

"Of course, kids," replied Pratham, "It's a long journey here, but getting home is a snap!"

"Thank you for all you've done for us," said Bandhu, "You changed our world with one simple sentence, 'Use your words!' Come back and visit us whenever you want."

"You're welcome!" said Ramesh.

"But now it's time to get back home!" Suresh said.

Pratham snapped his fingers. SNAP!

Ramesh and Suresh woke to find
themselves lying on Mom's lap with
her stroking their hair.

Happy and relieved, they jumped up
and gave her a big hug.

Mom asked, "What is it, kids?"

They smiled and said, "We love you, Mom! And we promise to use our words from now on!"

Then they ran outside to play Holi with their friends, and they carried with them a whole lot of words.

CAUTION: Never Cook without an Adult Supervision

Prep Time: 20min			
Cook Time: 20min		Serves 4	
Puri		Bhaji	
Whole wheat flour	1 cup	Potatoes	4-5 medium
Semolina	2 tablespoons	Oil	2 tablespoons
Salt	pinch	Mustard seeds	1/2 teaspoon
Oil	for cooking	Cumin seeds	1/2 teaspoon
		Asafoetida	pinch
		Curry leaves	6-8
		Green chillies slit	2-3
		Turmeric powder	1/4 teaspoon
		Salt	pinch
		Oil	for cooking

Make puri dough

- ☐ Put whole wheat flour in a large mixing bowl, add semolina, salt and oil and mix.
- ☐ Add enough water to knead into stiff dough.
- ☐ Cover the dough with a damp cloth and let it rest for 10 to 15 minutes.
- ☐ Divide the dough into small portions, roll it into balls and then roll it out into thick small discs.
- ☐ Heat enough oil to fry your discs, in a deep frying pan.
- ☐ Carefully slide into hot oil and deep-fry till golden brown and crisp. Drain on absorbent paper.

Make bhaji

- ☐ Heat oil in a non-stick pan, add mustard seeds and once they start to splutter, add asafoetida and cumin seeds.
- ☐ When the cumin seeds start to change color, add curry leaves and green chillies and sauté for a few seconds.
- ☐ Cut potatoes into cubes and add to the pan. Lightly mash potatoes with the back of a spoon, sprinkle some water and mix.
- ☐ Add half the coriander leaves and mix well.
- ☐ Cover and cook for two to three minutes.
- ☐ Transfer bhaji into a serving bowl and garnish with remaining coriander leaves.